Anansi and Brer Rabbit Stories

Retold by Pratima Mitchell

Contents

Longman

Edinburgh Gate
Harlow, Essex

Anansi, Lion and Mouse

A long time ago, Anansi the wise Spider lived in the
forest. He had many friends. He was a kind spider.
He liked to help his friends. One day he went for
a walk in the jungle. It was dark and spooky.
Suddenly Anansi the Spider jumped. A loud
noise was coming from deep in the jungle.

Anansi knew it was Lion. Lion was roaring very
loudly. Anansi looked in the jungle for Lion.

Lion's roars got louder and louder. At last
Anansi found Lion. Lion was sitting under a
big tree. Lion roared when he saw Anansi.
"Look what I have found," said Lion.

In Lion's paw there was a tiny mouse.
Mouse was Anansi's friend. Mouse
was crying.
"Help me, Anansi," cried Mouse. "Tell Lion
to let me go! I saved his life. Now he says
he will eat me."
"Help me Anansi!" said Mouse again.

"How did Lion catch you?" Anansi asked. Mouse told him his story. Mouse said he was looking for food in the jungle. He heard angry growls. He found Lion had fallen into a big hole. The big hole was a trap. Hunters had dug the big hole so they could catch Lion. Lion begged Mouse for help. Mouse felt very sorry for Lion. "I won't harm you, little Mouse. Please get me out of this hole. I will always be your friend."

Mouse tried to think how he could get Lion out. At last
he had a good idea. He cut a long jungle creeper with
his teeth. Slowly he pulled the creeper to the hole.
Mouse tied one end of the creeper to a big tree. The
other end of the creeper he let fall into the deep hole.

Lion took the creeper by his strong teeth. He held on
to the creeper and climbed out of the trap.
"Thank you Mouse," he said. "Thank you for helping
me." Then he put out his paw and grabbed hold of
Mouse. "I'm so sorry. I have not eaten for three days.
I am very hungry. I will have to eat you."
"Now he won't let me go. That's my story," said Mouse,
crying. "Oh save me please, Anansi my friend!"

Anansi the Spider knew he had to do something
quickly. At last he had an idea. "I say, Lion, you are so
big and strong. I don't believe that tiny little Mouse got
you out of a big deep hole."
Lion said, "Oh yes he did."
"Really?" asked Anansi. "Show me how."

Lion roared, "You don't believe me? Look, here is the
creeper." Lion showed Anansi the jungle creeper. "Can
you see how Mouse tied one end to that big tree over
there?" Lion showed Anansi the big tree. "Then Mouse
pulled the other end of the creeper and gave it to me."
Lion jumped into the deep hole. "Then I held the
creeper and climbed out. Look, this is how I did it!"

But while Lion was talking to Anansi, Mouse was busy.
Lion was telling Anansi how he had got out of the
deep hole. He didn't see what Mouse was up to.
Mouse quickly ate through the jungle creeper. Now the
creeper was not tied to the big tree any more. When
Lion tried to climb out of the hole again, he fell back.
Kerplunk!

Lion roared and roared! "Get me out of here, little
Mouse! Get me out, friend Anansi!"

But Anansi and Mouse were far away by then.

"Thank you, dear Anansi, for saving my life," Mouse
said. "I will go and find some jungle plums for you."
Mouse said, "You will always be my very best friend."
Anansi rubbed his tummy. He felt very happy. He had
helped Mouse and now he was going to get his
favourite fruit to eat.

Brer Rabbit and the Little Girl

Once upon a time Brer Rabbit went for a walk. He went past a pretty little garden. Round the garden was a fence.

In the fence there was a gate. Brer Rabbit looked through the fence. He could smell something green and fresh. He had a nose for green and fresh things. Somewhere in that pretty garden there was lettuce. He just knew it!

Brer Rabbit looked this way and that. He tried to see through the fence. Then he rubbed his eyes. There on the far side were rows and rows of lettuce. Brer Rabbit had never seen so much lettuce in his life! But he couldn't open the gate. How was he going to get to that lettuce?

Then Brer Rabbit saw a little girl coming down the road. He hid behind a bush. The little girl opened the gate. She went inside the pretty garden. She went to the rows of lettuce. She cut a nice fat lettuce and popped it into her bag.

Now Brer Rabbit had a plan. Next morning he met the little girl on the road.
"Good morning, missy."
"Good morning," replied the little girl. Brer Rabbit smiled at her.
"I met your daddy just now. He said you could open the gate for me. Your daddy said I could eat his lettuce."

The little girl said, "Oh, Brer Rabbit, if Daddy said so ..." She opened the gate and Brer Rabbit shot inside. He ran to the far side of the garden. He began to eat.

He ate and he ate. He ate up a whole row of fresh green lettuce. He was so full he could hardly walk!

Next day the little girl opened the gate for him again. Again Brer Rabbit went for the lettuce. He ate and ate until he was going to burst!

9

The day after that the little girl's daddy came to his garden. He wanted to weed the lettuce. Then he let out a cry. "What has happened to my lettuce? Who has been eating my lettuce?"

The little girl said, "Oh Daddy, that was Brer Rabbit. He said you told him I could open the gate for him." Well, her daddy was very angry.
"Brer Rabbit told you a big lie. I am going to punish him."

Next morning Brer Rabbit came to the garden. The little girl opened the gate for him. But there was a nasty shock for Brer Rabbit! The little girl's daddy picked up Brer Rabbit by his neck. "You lying thief! I'll teach you to steal my lettuce."
"Sorry Mr Man," said Brer Rabbit. "It's no good saying that now," said Mr Man. He tied up Brer Rabbit's paws so he couldn't run away. "You wait here. I'll come back and punish you some more," said Mr Man.

10

Brer Rabbit was in big trouble. What was he going to do? Well, what do you think he did? He started to sing! Brer Rabbit had a lovely voice. He sang so well that the little girl clapped.
"You have such a lovely voice, Brer Rabbit," she said.

"Oh, do you really think so?" Brer Rabbit sang her another song. Then he sang another.
"Will you give me singing lessons, Brer Rabbit?" asked the little girl.
"Of course I will," said Brer Rabbit. "But little girl, if you think I sing so well you should see me dance!"
"Oh really, Brer Rabbit – can you dance?"

"I'd be happy to show you," said Brer Rabbit. He held out his paws. "I'm sorry I can't dance right now. Just see how your daddy has tied me up."

The little girl said, "Don't worry about that. Here, let me untie you." She quickly untied Brer Rabbit's paws. He was free! With one big hop he was out of the gate. With another big hop he was on his way. As he ran down the road he called, "Tell your daddy his lettuce is the best I've ever tasted!"

King Bird's Party

Once upon a time, long ago, the King of the Birds had a birthday. He wanted to give a party. He wanted a very big party. The King of the Birds said, "I want to have my party at home. I will have a tree party."

He said, "It costs too much money to take my friends to MacBird's. We can all meet at the top of the big oak tree. We will have a party on top of the big oak tree. All the birds can fly there." His wife, the Queen of the Birds asked, "What about a fancy dress party?"

The King of the Birds replied, "What a good idea! I will go as a Space Bird." The Queen of the Birds said, "And I will go as a Spice Bird."

12

The King of the Birds said, "I want lots and lots and lots of presents. I want balloons and paper hats. And we will play *lots* of games. I will win all the games and get all the prizes!"

"Yes, dear," said the Queen of the Birds. "Now what about food? What shall we give your friends?" The King of the Birds said, "All the things I like best – yummy worm pie, bread pudding, baked nuts and coconut ice-cream."

Anansi the Spider heard about King Bird's party. "I want to go to the party," said Anansi the Spider. Robin said, "Spiders can't go to King Bird's party. This party is only for birds."
"I'll go if I want," said Anansi. "I will dress up as a bird and go to the party."

Anansi knew there would be loads of food at King Bird's party. Anansi liked to eat everything.

He loved cakes and crisps and sweets and ice-cream. And he also loved worm pie and bread pudding. Anansi just loved to eat. When he thought about the party his mouth began to water.

He visited each bird in turn and asked them to lend him one of their feathers. First he went to the crow. Then he went to the robin. Next he went to the blue jay. All the birds in the forest gave him a feather from their tails. Then Anansi rolled himself in some honey which he got from the bees. He stuck feathers all over himself. He was covered in feathers.

Everyone looked at Anansi. They had never seen such
a strange-looking bird. His wife said, "The King of the
Birds is having a *fancy* dress party." Anansi said, "*This* is
fancy dress for me! I'm going as a bird. Look at me!"
He flapped his wings. He jumped up a little. He was
able to jump high. All the feathers on his sticky little
body lifted him up.

Then Anansi jumped even higher. The wind got under
all his stuck-on feathers. The wind lifted him to the first
branch of the big oak tree. Then Anansi jumped once
more. This time the wind took him to the top of the tree.

The big oak tree was full of green and red balloons.
All the birds were there. All the birds were in fancy
dress. Everyone was singing. It was very noisy. King
Bird came as a Space Bird. He wore a silver space
suit. Queen Bird came as a Spice Bird so she wore a
yellow wig.

King Bird looked at Anansi. "Who are you?" he asked.
"I've come as You All."
"You All? You All? I've never heard of You All. Who is
You All?" "Oh, he's very, very famous," said Anansi.
"Happy Birthday, Your Majesty."

Then came the food. Anansi licked his lips. "Come on you all," cried the King of the Birds. "You all! Come on and eat," said King Bird and Queen Bird.

Anansi took the worm pie. He ate it all up. He grabbed the coconut ice-cream. He ate up the nuts. Anansi ate quickly. No food was left for any of the other birds.

"What are you doing," they cried. "Leave us some pie! Leave us some nuts!" Anansi said, "King Bird said, come on you all. My name is You All. All the food is for me!" Then all the birds fell on Anansi. They pulled off his feathers. It was so cold up on the big oak tree! Anansi could not fly down. He could not get away quickly enough. "You greedy spider!" the King of Birds said. "Don't come here again!"

Anansi ran away home and hid under his bed. The King of the Birds had to take all the birds to MacBird's in the end. There they had worm-burgers and milk shakes. They had a very good time after all.

Anansi was so full that he slept for three days!

Brer Rabbit Goes Fishing

There was a time when Brer Rabbit was best
friends with Brer Turtle. They had a lot
of fun. They went for picnics.
They played hide-and-seek
in the woods. They played
tricks on the other animals.
Then how they laughed,
ha-ha, hee-hee!

One day Brer Rabbit came
to Brer Turtle and said
"Brer Turtle, now you *are*
my best friend, aren't you?"
"Oh yes, Brer Rabbit.
There's no one else I have so
much fun with."
Brer Rabbit said in a whisper. "Will you help me then?"
"Of course. No problem," replied Brer Turtle.
"Truth is, Brer Turtle, I have a few enemies. Brer Fox,
Brer Wolf and Brer Bear have all been mean to me,"
Brer Rabbit said to Brer Turtle. "Okay, Brer Rabbit.
How can we punish Brer Fox, Brer Wolf and Brer Bear?"

Brer Rabbit grinned. "We'll go fishing!"
"Fishing, Brer Rabbit?" Brer Turtle looked puzzled.
"Yes, fishing! We'll go fishing in Mud Pond. You just
have to do just what I say. Don't ask me any more.
Just do as I tell you and we'll have a big laugh."
Brer Turtle smiled. "Good, let's go."

17

The two friends got together their fishing rods, lines and nets. They strolled down to the woods, laughing and talking very loudly. All the creatures heard them talking about the fish they were going to catch. It tickled Brer Fox's fancy so he felt like going fishing too.
"Hey, can I go fishing with you fellows?" he called.
"Of couse you can," Brer Rabbit replied. So Brer Fox joined the two friends. All three strolled down to Mud Pond.

Next Brer Wolf met them along the way.
"Hey, can I go with you?" he called.
"Sure thing, Brer Wolf," cried Brer Rabbit merrily. Now Brer Wolf joined Brer Rabbit, Brer Turtle and Brer Fox. They all strolled down to Mud Pond, laughing and talking.

Then it was Brer Bear's turn.
"Hey, can I go fishing with you?" called Brer Bear.
"Why not?" cried Brer Rabbit. So now Brer Bear joined Brer Rabbit, Brer Turtle, Brer Fox and Brer Wolf and they all walked down to Mud Pond together.

There was Mud Pond before them. It was evening and the Moon was floating in the sky. Brer Rabbit got his rod and line ready. He hooked a piece of bread on the end of his line. He cast the line into the still water.
Splash! Brer Rabbit gave a little skip and shouted, "Look out!" The others were unpacking their gear. They had spread their nets and jam jars on the banks of Mud Pond.
"What's up, Brer Rabbit?" they called.

"Oh my, oh my. Don't even ask!" cried Brer Rabbit. Brer Turtle hurried up to see.
"Look, Brer Turtle! Look, the Moon's gone and fallen into Mud Pond," said Brer Rabbit sadly.
"Oh my, oh my, oh my. Whatever are we going to do?" Brer Rabbit winked at Brer Turtle.
"Oh my, oh my, oh my," cried Brer Turtle.

Brer Fox, Brer Wolf and Brer Bear came to the edge of the water. There was the silver Moon floating on the pond. "Oh my, oh my, oh my," they all cried.

"There's only one thing to do," Brer Rabbit said. "We must rescue the Moon, or the whole world will be in trouble." "Get your nets everyone. Let's go and get the Moon before she drowns!"

Brer Fox, Brer Wolf and Brer Bear fetched their nets and waded into Mud Pond. Brer Rabbit and Brer Turtle stayed on the shore to watch. The water came up to their knees. They threw out their nets and tried to pull in the Moon. They tried again and again, but they couldn't get hold of her.

"Go in deeper. That's right, deeper still," Brer Rabbit said. Brer Fox, Brer Wolf and Brer Bear waded deeper into Mud Pond. Now they were up to their waists. Soon, in no time at all, the water had reached their chests. Then they were in so deep that the water reached their chins.

Still the Moon refused to be caught. Meanwhile Brer Turtle was standing by the water's edge killing himself laughing.

Suddenly, Brer Fox, Brer Wolf and Brer Bear slipped
and went right under.

"*Splutter, splutter, splutter,*" they gasped, spitting out
gallons of dirty water.

"Ha-ha-ha, hee-hee-hee!" Brer Fox, Brer Wolf and
Brer Bear saw Brer Rabbit and Brer Turtle rolling on
the grass, gasping for breath. They were laughing
hard as hard could be. The two friends looked up and
pointed to the Moon high above, safe in the sky. Then
Brer Rabbit and Brer Turtle picked themselves up,
turned round and ran back home, dancing all the way.

"That'll teach you to be mean to Brer Rabbit," they
called as they disappeared into the woods. Brer Fox,
Brer Wolf and Brer Bear climbed out of Mud Pond,
dripping wet.

"A-tishoo! *A-tishoo!* A-tishoo!" All three went home
without any fish. But they all did catch a cold instead.

Anansi and the Magic Spell

Many long years ago, Anansi
the Spider got into bad, bad
trouble. It had to happen
sooner or later. Clever he
was, but *too* clever. Lazy
he was, oh lazy to his
smallest bone. Greedy he
was too, because he just
loved to eat and eat.
Anansi was a clever, lazy,
greedy spider, and that's just
the way he was made.

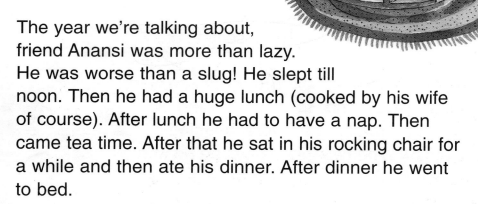

The year we're talking about,
friend Anansi was more than lazy.
He was worse than a slug! He slept till
noon. Then he had a huge lunch (cooked by his wife
of course). After lunch he had to have a nap. Then
came tea time. After that he sat in his rocking chair for
a while and then ate his dinner. After dinner he went
to bed.

Before the Moon could raise her chin above the trees,
Anansi was fast asleep and snoring. That year we're
talking of, he hardly worked at all. He didn't dig, or
plant, or weed. There was nothing in his field. Nothing!
Not even a small bean plant.

Now, I hear you thinking, how did Anansi, his wife and children eat? Where did the food come from? The tasty sweet potatoes, the foo-foo, the spinach in red palm oil, the banana chips, the sticky rice? It came from the grocery store. The grocery store was only a scuttle away.

Now, I hear you thinking, how did he buy the food? Where did the money come from? Well now, Anansi was clever. He sweet-talked his way into getting a pound here, a pound there. He borrowed money from his friends. The lion, the python, the alligator, they all lent him money. That suited him very well, until one day his friends wanted their money back.

The lion, the python, the alligator came to Anansi's door. "I need my money for a haircut," roared the lion. "I'm going on holiday," hissed the python. "I'm building a beach hut," croaked the alligator. "It's time you paid us back," they all said.

Anansi smiled at his friends. "Why do you worry? I'll pay you back tomorrow." But Anansi had no idea how he would do that. Because Anansi was so worried, he spun one cobweb and then another and then another. Soon the whole forest was covered in cobwebs. He could not stop worrying about how he was going to pay back the money. His wife said, "You are wasting your energy spinning and spinning cobwebs. Go and talk to the wise tortoise about your problem. He may have a good idea."

"I owe money to the lion, the python and the alligator," Anansi told the tortoise. "Can you help me?" The tortoise, who was a wise old creature, said "I know some magic, but it will cost you."
"I promise I'll work day and night on my farm," Anansi said. "I promise that in three months I'll be able to sell my crops and pay you."

The tortoise stared hard at Anansi. (Tortoises don't blink, as you know.) "All right then. Drink this magic drink. Now, when your friends come to you for their money, this is what you say: 'Go jump in the river!' Then you laugh loudly: 'Ha-ha-ha-ha, hoo-hoo-hoo-hoo!' Watch what happens next. They will start laughing after you. They will laugh so hard that they'll forget all about the money that you owe them."

Anansi returned home and sure enough the lion came knocking at his door. "Huh," said Anansi. "Go jump in the river!" Then he started to laugh: "Ha-ha-ha-ha, hoo-hoo-hoo-hoo!" He laughed and laughed.

It was catching. The lion started to laugh with him: "Ha-ha-ha-ha, hoo-hoo-hoo-hoo!" He laughed and laughed and couldn't stop. Sure enough, he forgot all about the money and went off into the forest still laughing loudly.

Then the python turned up asking for his money. Exactly the same thing happened with him. "Go jump in the river!" said Anansi boldly and started to laugh. The python couldn't help laughing as well. Very soon he turned around and went back into the forest, still laughing loudly.

Last of all came the alligator. "Go jump in the river!" Anansi said and laughed: "Ha-ha-ha-ha, hoo-hoo-hoo-hoo!" The alligator went off laughing as well, never thinking about the money he was owed.

Anansi was very happy. The magic had worked. There was enough food in the cupboard and it was time for a little nap again. But the tortoise did not forget that Anansi still had to pay him for his good idea. He came round one day looking for his money. Of course Anansi had none to give him.

"I'll play the same trick on the old tortoise," thought clever Anansi. "Go jump in the river!" he shouted. Then he began laughing: "Ha-ha-ha-ha, hoo-hoo-hoo-hoo!" His laugh was so catching that the tortoise couldn't help laughing as well. "Ha-ha-ha-ha, hoo-hoo-hoo-hoo!" he went. He laughed and laughed and couldn't stop to draw breath. Still laughing, he made his way back into the forest. Clever Anansi. What a trickster!

Brer Rabbit's Race

Far away and long ago, Brer Rabbit also knew someone who carted his house around wherever he went. His name was Brer Turtle. Brer Rabbit liked showing off in front of Brer Turtle.

Brer Turtle was slow. He took his time over things. "Let me see now ... umm," and "take it easy" he was fond of saying. This made Brer Rabbit want to run and jump and spring up and race round. He wanted to show that he was a fit and fast rabbit. So much fitter and faster than poor, slow Brer Turtle.

"Oh, stop showing off, Brer Rabbit!" said Brer Turtle. "What are you trying to prove? I can beat you in a race any time at all."
"Get away!" said Brer Rabbit, panting as he rushed up a hill, rushed down again and lickety-split around the meadow.

"No, no, I'm serious," Brer Turtle said. "Just slow down for a minute and I'll tell you what I have in mind."

"Yes, go on," and Brer Rabbit, turning three cartwheels before landing neatly on his feet. Then he rolled over on his back and did some bicycling exercises.

Brer Turtle felt dizzy watching him. "Take it easy now, I said. I want to race you," he said in his quiet way. Brer Rabbit started laughing so hard that he couldn't do his bicycling exercises. His legs slowed down and finally stopped going round and round.

"You what?" he spluttered, gasping for breath.

"I want to race you!" said Brer Turtle.

"Never! You wouldn't have the nerve!"

"I'll bet you a sackful of lettuce that I'll win the race too."

"Brer Turtle, Brer Turtle, don't say what you might regret. You know I'm so fit and fast that they begged me not to enter the Olympics. The whole world knew I would win," boasted Brer Rabbit.

"You won't win this race, Brer Rabbit. Not this race," Brer Turtle chuckled. Brer Rabbit did not believe him.

"Okay, if you say so. Why should I turn down a sackful of juicy lettuce? I'm going to win this race. Easy-peasy. Come on, let's go!"

It was agreed that the race would take place the next week. The starting point would be the old oak tree. Brer Rabbit and Brer Turtle would follow the path through the wood, right up to the stream on the other side. The race was three miles. Every half a mile there would be a post to show how far they had run.

Brer Rabbit went into training. He did his push-ups and his jogging-on-the-spot. He went to bed early and ate lots of extra carrots.

Brer Turtle did nothing. That's right, nothing. He went about his normal life – going to work, taking the kids to school, helping his wife. He wasn't bothered about the race. He knew he was going to win. He had a trick up his sleeve.

All turtles look the same. Have you noticed, you can't tell one from the other? On the morning of the race, Brer Turtle put his wife at the starting line. At each of the six posts he put one of his children. His children hid under bushes so they couldn't be seen.

The race began! Brer Fox banged on a drum and they were off! Except it was Mrs Turtle and not Brer Turtle who started off with Brer Rabbit running on ahead. Since she looked exactly like Brer Turtle, nobody could tell it was she and not her husband.

When Brer Rabbit reached the first post, he ran past it and looked round. There was Brer Turtle right behind him! Except now it wasn't Brer Turtle, but son number one.

At the second post Brer Turtle's son number two crawled out from under a bush. When Brer Rabbit turned round, there was son number two just keeping up with him. But it looked to Brer Rabbit that Brer Turtle was just behind him. Brer Rabbit was panting and sweating and running at a great speed, lickety-split, lickety split. He wondered how could Brer Turtle look so cool and calm?

At the third post Brer Turtle's oldest daughter crawled out from under a bush. She too looked just like Brer Turtle.It seemed like Brer Turtle was still keeping up with Brer Rabbit. And so it went – right up until the fifth post.

Brer Turtle's sons and daughters crawled out of the bushes just before Brer Rabbit was due to run past each of the six posts. Brer Rabbit of course thought that Brer Turtle was keeping up with him.

Of course he was faster than Brer Turtle. But not that much faster, it seemed. He was going to win the race! *Of course* he was going to win the race. He was a champion runner; the fastest creature in the forest.

At the sixth and last post, Brer Turtle himself crawled out of a thick holly bush. He went and touched the finishing line easily, a good minute before Brer Rabbit came running up towards it. "I've won, Brer Rabbit!" said Brer Turtle, all cool as a blade of grass with the dew still on it. "I'm the winner of the race and you owe me a sackful of juicy lettuce," said Brer Turtle. Brer Rabbit flopped out, sweating and panting, too tired to answer him. "Puff-puff-puff-puff! How did I lose the race?" he wondered.

To the end of his days he kept wondering how did Brer Turtle manage to beat him? Well, you know, and I know, and we can keep a secret, can't we?